NURSERY RHYMES FOR TRUMPIAN TIMES

by Mukesh Sahu

Nursery Rhymes for Trumpian Times

ISBN: 978-1-7343169-2-6

Published by Samsara Publications

For my precious V & S.
May you soon live in a world where this all remains but a distant memory...

No one could argue that the hallmark of Donald Trump's tenure over the last three years has been his unprecedented defiance of political and social norms. One of the more concerning consequences of this conduct, and the driving force behind this book, is the progressive normalization of words and actions that were once universally condemned as unacceptable. There existed a time not long ago when a single questionable statement by an elected official precipitated a swift fall from power. No longer. Today, Trump's barrage of drivel wears down our defenses and renders us numb.

It is tempting to simply accept this as the new normal—it is certainly easier and much less demoralizing to do so. But as principled, feeling human beings and citizens of the world, we must resist this temptation.

These reimagined nursery rhymes therefore constitute my small contribution to that resistance. It is an unconventional format to be sure, but because these classics cast a spell via their instantly recognizable lines and characters, they will hopefully resonate with you on a deeper, more personal level. In addition, while the book's content does not focus exclusively on Trump, it is my hope that those particular portions supplement the outstanding work already being carried out by journalists, satirists, political commentators, late-night talk show hosts, and the multitude of private citizens that every day take to the streets, social media, and seats of government to hold this administration accountable for its actions.

In the end, whatever your social leanings or political ideology, I hope at the very least these rhymes and images offer you another perspective on the extraordinary events unfolding before our eyes from the confines of the Oval Office to the furthest reaches of the globe. If this collection manages to accomplish this for even one person, I will consider it a resounding success.

-M.S.

Table of Contents

BAA BAA BLACK SHEEP

Baa baa black sheep

Have you any worth?

No sir, no sir,

You are dirt.

We the white masters

Were born to reign

This is our America

We'll make it great again

TRUMP
-2020-
KEEP AMERICA GREAT!

TRUMPTY DUMBTY (ORIGINALLY HUMPTY DUMPTY)

Trumpty Dumbty wanted a wall

To keep out the Mexicans once and for all

He stole kids from parents to lock them in cages

And labeled them murderers, animals, and rapists

11

I'M A LITTLE CRACKPOT (ORIGINALLY I'M A LITTLE TEAPOT)

I'm a little crackpot, short and stout

Not very bright but I have a big mouth

When my Twitter feed's on, SEE ME SHOUT

Do the world a favor and force me out

THERE WAS AN OLD WOMAN WHO LIVED IN A SHOE

There was an old woman who lived in a shoe

She had so many children she didn't know what to do

Barred access to birth control thanks to right-wing nonsense

She bore and raised all of them, at taxpayers' expense

Planned Parenthood

45

IT'S RAINING, IT'S POURING

It's raining, it's pouring

The old man is snoring

He went to sleep, while the levee breached

And had no home in the morning

ROW ROW ROW YOUR BOAT

Row, row, row your boat

Quickly down the street

Steadily, steadily, steadily, steadily,

Higher rise the seas

JACK AND JILL

Jack and Jill went up the hill

To fetch a pail of water

Jill soon learned, versus Jack she earned

Just seventy cents on the dollar

WEE WILLY WINKY

Wee Willie Winky runs through the town

Upstairs and downstairs in his nightgown

Though he's an asset on the field of battle

He's no longer allowed, given his "alternative" lifestyle

ARMY

GEORGY PORGY

Georgy Porgy, pudding and pie

Kissed the girls and made them cry

They stood tall and screamed #MeToo!

And Georgy Porgy got his due

23

DON, DON FRED'S MIDDLE SON
(ORIGINALLY TOM, TOM, THE PIPER'S SON)

Don, Don, Fred's middle son

Bankrupted casinos and away did run

Failures complete, and Don was beat

Until he stole the presidency

LIQUIDATION SALE
TAJ MAHAL HOTEL
MAHAL
Pennsylvania AV NW

THE QUEEN OF HEARTS

The Queen of Hearts

She made some tarts,

All on a summer's day;

The Knave of Hearts

He stole those tarts,

And took them clean away;

The King of Hearts

Called for the tarts,

And beat the knave full sore;

Then shot at his heart

Despite raised arms

His skin was black in color

BLACK LIVES MATTER

PUSSY CAT PUSSY CAT

Pussy cat, pussy cat,

Where have you been?

In Trump's tiny hand

Without permission

Pussy cat, pussy cat,

What did you there?

I suffered in silence

Till his voice ran on air

DING DONG BELL

Ding, dong, bell

Pussy's gonna tell

Who grabbed her up?

Dirty Donald Trump

Who got the push?

Complicit Billy Bush

What a naughty boy was that

That tried to grab poor pussy cat

Believing his celebrity

Lent license to misogyny

OLD MACDONALD

Old Macdonald's factory farm

E-I-E-I-O

And on this farm are many pigs

E-I-E-I-O

With a conveyor belt here, a decapitator there

Here a head, there a head, every second another head

Old Macdonald's factory farm

It's a horror show

ROCK A BYE BABY

Rock a bye baby, on the treetop

Taking a stand, and striving to stop

The plunder of nature from mountain to sea

She'll fight and she'll win against corporate greed

33

RUB A DUB DUB 1

Rub a dub dub, three men in a tub

And how do you think they got there?

Trump, Cohen, Roger Stone

Obstructing justice while on the throne (allegedly)

'Twas enough to make patriots despair

RUB A DUB DUB 2

Rub a dub dub, two men in a tub

And how do you think they got there?

Donald Trump, with Vladimir Putin

Stood in a shower of golden urine

(At least per the Steele Dossier)

PEEPEE TAPE

PAT A CAKE

Pat a cake, pat a cake, baker's man

Bake me a cake as fast as you can

Design it, and ice it, and top it with two brides

You say you can refuse? We'll have the courts decide.

THERE WAS A CROOKED MAN

There was a crooked man

With a crooked business style

He called her crooked Hillary,

Yet was crooked all the while

He ran a crooked House

With countless crooked aides

Maintained his crooked path

Through his final crooked days

FOX
NEWS
LOCK
HER UP!

LITTLE MIKE PENCE (ORIGINALLY LITTLE BO PEEP)

Little Mike Pence has lost his sense

For with women he never alone dines

And if alcohol flows, he is a no-show

Unless his wifey stands at his side

43

JACK SPRAT

Jack Sprat could eat no fat

His wife could eat no lean

Obamacare put cures in reach

Then Trump got in between

24-HR PHARMACY
OBAMACARE
APPLY TODAY

THE ITSY BITSY SPIDER

The itsy bitsy spider climbed up the waterspout

Down came the rain and washed the spider out

On came the floods, then the drought, then more rain

Extreme is now the normal, thanks to climate change

HUSH LITTLE BABY

Hush little baby, don't say a word

Mama's gonna buy you a mockingbird

And if that mockingbird won't sing

Mama's gonna buy you a diamond ring

And if that diamond ring turns brass

Mama's gonna buy you a looking glass

And on and on and on it goes

Buy, discard, and buy some more

Reckless, wasteful consumption

Our legacy for future generations

Please little baby, don't hate us

Even though we've betrayed your trust

We're short-sighted, selfish fools

But there's still hope, we still have you

TWINKLE, TWINKLE

Twinkle, twinkle shining star

How I wonder where you are

On a hill, you were our guide

Now you hate, betray, divide

Twinkle, twinkle shining star

How I wonder where you are

AN ELEPHANT TALKS (ORIGINALLY AN ELEPHANT WALKS)

An elephant talks about this and that

He's terribly small and he's terribly fat

He has no brain,

He has no heart,

And we'll rise from the ashes

When at last he departs

www.ingramcontent.com/pod-product-compliance
Lightning Source LLC
Chambersburg PA
CBHW041138100726

47911CB00005B/146